To Jessica from
Grandmom and Grandpop.
Merry Christmas 1996.

Classic Fairy Tales

Classic Fairy Tales

Edited by Armand Eisen

BARNES
&NOBLE
BOOKS
NEW YORK

Originally published as *The Classic Fairy Tale Treasury*
© 1991, 1992, and 1995 by Armand Eisen
This edition published by Barnes & Noble, Inc.,
by arrangement with Andrews and McMeel
1996 Barnes & Noble Books
ISBN-0-7607-0398-1

Contents

The Classic Fairy Tale Treasury

BEAUTY and the BEAST

Retold by SAMANTHA EASTON

Illustrated by RUTH SANDERSON

$\mathcal{T}$here was once a rich merchant who through no fault of his own lost his entire fortune. All he had left was a small house in the country where he and his family would now have to live.

The merchant had three daughters. The youngest was so lovely that everyone called her Beauty.

The merchant had always given his daughters the best of everything, and the two eldest girls were very spoiled. They hated their new home and did nothing but complain about it. Beauty, however, tried to make the best of things.

A year had passed in this way when the merchant received some good news. One of his ships, which he had believed lost, had come into port with all its cargo safe and sound.

Beauty's sisters were overjoyed. They were sure the family would soon be as rich as before. As their father prepared to leave for town, they begged him to bring them back fine silk dresses and jeweled necklaces.

But Beauty asked for nothing.

The merchant noticed her silence. "How about you, Beauty? What would you like?"

"I only wish you to come home safely, Father," the girl replied.

"But there must be something I can bring you," said Beauty's father.

"Very well," she said. "Bring me a rose. None grow here, and I am so fond of them."

So the merchant set off for town. When he arrived he learned that all the cargo had been stolen. There was nothing for him to do but turn around and head home.

When the merchant was only a few miles from home, a terrible storm blew up. The snow fell so heavily that the merchant could not go on. He looked for shelter, but there was none in the forest. He was growing desperate when he spotted a path through the trees. He steered his horse onto it.

As he went down the path the snow cleared and the air grew warmer. Soon the merchant was on a paved road. On either side were orange trees heavy with ripe fruit. "How strange!" he thought. He kept going until he came to a white marble palace.

The gates were open and the palace was entirely lit. The merchant wandered through the rooms, but he could find no one at home. He stopped in a room with a blazing fire. Thinking the fire must have been made for someone who would soon appear, he sat down before it and fell asleep.

The merchant awoke in the morning to find a full breakfast set out for him. He hungrily devoured it, then walked through the palace once again looking for his mysterious host. But he could find no one. Finally he decided to be on his way and went outside to find his horse.

In the garden the merchant saw a rose bush covered with beautiful flowers. "At least, I can bring Beauty her gift," he thought as he plucked one.

Then, a terrible voice above him said, "Thief! Is this how you repay the Beast's kindness? That rose will cost you your life!"

The merchant turned to see a fearsome beast looming over him. "Please forgive me, sir," he cried, falling to his knees. "I only wished to bring a rose to my daughter, Beauty." Then he told the Beast his story.

When the merchant had finished, the Beast said, "Very well, I will spare your life, but one of your daughters must agree to take your place!"

The merchant was horrified. But he accepted the condition, and the Beast let him go still carrying the rose for Beauty.

When the merchant reached home, his daughters eagerly ran to meet him. He gave them the sad news that he was as poor as ever. Then he handed Beauty her rose. "Here is what you asked for," he sighed, "but you cannot imagine what it cost!"

His daughters asked him to explain.

Upon hearing his story, the two older daughters turned on Beauty. "It is all your fault," they said. "You had to ask for a rose, and now look what you have done!"

"I know," Beauty replied. "And so it is only fair that I go to the Beast in my father's place." Her father said he would not allow her to do this, but Beauty stood firm. After a week had passed, Beauty and her father set out for the Beast's palace.

The journey passed quickly. Soon they were walking down the road lined with orange trees. Although Beauty was frightened, she could not help marveling at the Beast's gardens. They were full of fruit and flowers even though it was winter.

As before, the palace was beautifully lit, but there was no one to be seen. Inside, a fire blazed in the same room, and a big meal had been set out. But Beauty and her father were both too upset to eat. After a while, the door opened and in walked the Beast.

The Beast was horrible to look at, but Beauty greeted him politely. He asked her if she had come willingly, and she replied in a steady voice, "Yes, Beast."

The Beast then told the merchant to go home, and he gave him two chests of gold to take with him. Beauty and her father thought they would never see each other again. They embraced and the merchant reluctantly rode away.

Beauty expected the Beast to kill her at once, but he left her alone. When it grew dark, Beauty found herself before a room with her name written above it in gold letters.

The room had a graceful bed and a matching dressing table. The wardrobe was full of lovely gowns. "Surely, the Beast would not give me these things if he meant to kill me," Beauty thought. Then, feeling much better, she fell asleep.

The next morning, Beauty awoke to find breakfast set out for her. All day long she amused herself by wandering through the palace. Sometimes she heard music and voices, but she saw no one.

When evening came Beauty found a delicious supper waiting for her in her room. She was just sitting down to eat, when the Beast knocked at her door. "Beauty," he said softly. "May I please watch you eat?"

Beauty trembled with fear, but she replied bravely, "Yes, Beast."

So the Beast sat beside her, and they spoke of many things. To Beauty's surprise, the Beast was a pleasant companion. But at the end of the meal, the Beast asked, "Do you love me, Beauty? Will you marry me?"

"How can I answer?" Beauty said.

"Tell the truth," replied the Beast.

"Then, no, dear Beast," Beauty replied gently. "I cannot marry you."

"Very well," the Beast said sadly.

Every night the Beast asked Beauty the same question. And even though she refused him, he treated her very kindly.

Soon Beauty began to enjoy living in the palace. Whenever she wished for anything—some embroidery thread or a kitten to keep her company—her wish was granted at once. She also grew very fond of the Beast, who was kind and generous to her. Despite his dreadful appearance, Beauty looked forward to the evenings when he would sit with her.

Yet Beauty missed her family, especially her dear father, and she slowly grew pale and ill from longing. At last, the Beast asked her what was wrong.

"I only wish I could see my family again, dear Beast," Beauty replied.

The Beast sighed. "If you go," he said mournfully, "it will be the death of me!"

"But I will only go for a month," Beauty promised. "Then I will come back and stay with you always."

"Then go," said the Beast. "But be sure to keep your promise or you will find me dead."

The Beast gave Beauty a silver ring and told her to put it on that night and wish she were home. "Tomorrow morning you will be there," the Beast said. "And when you wish to come back to me, put the ring on your finger when you go to bed. Then turn it once, and say, 'I wish to be with my dear Beast again.' By morning you will be here."

That night Beauty filled a trunk with gifts for her father and sisters. Then she put on the ring and wished herself home.

The next morning she was there. Her father was overjoyed. Her sisters pretended they were, too. But secretly they were jealous of Beauty, because the Beast had given her many expensive and beautiful things.

One day Beauty carelessly told them that she had promised the Beast to return in a month. "Let us make her stay longer," said one of her sisters. "Then the Beast may get angry with her and not let her come back."

When it came time for Beauty to go, her sisters burst into tears. "If you leave, we shall die of grief," they wailed. So Beauty stayed one day and then another and another, but she began to worry about the Beast.

One night, Beauty had a terrible dream. In it the Beast appeared before her and said, "Beauty, you broke your promise and now I shall die!"

Terrified, Beauty woke with a start. She placed the ring on her finger, turned it once, and said, "I wish to be back with my dear Beast again."

The next morning Beauty was in the Beast's palace. All day she waited for evening when the Beast would visit her. But evening came, and the Beast did not appear.

Beauty ran through the palace calling his name, to no avail. Next, she ran into the garden. There, she saw the Beast lying very still beneath the rose bushes.

Beauty ran to him. "He is dead," she sobbed, "and it is all because of me!" Just then the Beast's eyes opened. "Oh, Beast!" Beauty cried. "I am so glad you are still alive. I never knew how much I loved you until this moment!"

"Can you really love an ugly beast like myself?" the Beast asked.

"Yes," Beauty replied.

"Will you marry me, Beauty?"

"Yes, I will, dear Beast!"

Then there was a bright flash of light, and the Beast vanished. In his place stood a handsome prince. He told Beauty he had been placed under a spell by a wicked fairy. He was doomed to remain in the form of a hideous beast until some maiden should fall in love with him. Beauty's love had broken the spell, and now the prince wished to marry her.

The prince took Beauty back to the palace and introduced her to his mother and father, who under the wicked fairy's spell had been invisible.

Then Beauty sent for her father and her sisters. She told them of the prince's spell and the coming wedding. And so the marriage of Beauty and her prince was celebrated with great joy, and they lived happily ever after.

RUMPELSTILTSKIN

By THE BROTHERS GRIMM

Retold by JENNIFER GREENWAY

Illustrated by GARY COOLEY

*O*nce long ago there lived a miller who had a beautiful daughter. One day the king of the land happened to be passing by the mill. To make himself seem important to the king, the miller boasted that his daughter knew how to spin straw into gold.

The king, who liked gold very much, was most impressed.

"I should like to meet this daughter of yours," the king said to the miller. "Bring her to my palace tomorrow morning, and we shall see if what you say is true."

When the miller told his daughter what he had done, she was very upset. But there was nothing she could do. So early the next morning she presented herself at the king's palace.

The king led her into a large room that was completely filled with straw. Then he showed her to a spinning wheel and said, "Now you must get to work. But first, let me tell you this. If you have not spun all the straw into gold by tomorrow morning, you will pay with your life." Then the king left the room and locked the door behind him.

As soon as the king was gone, the miller's

beautiful daughter began to cry, despairing that she had no idea how to spin straw into gold. Just as she was sure there was no hope for her, the door of the room creaked open.

A strange little man came walking in. He looked at her and said, "Tell me, miller's daughter, why are you crying?"

"The king has ordered me to spin this straw into gold," she sobbed. "Unless I do he will have me put to death. And I have no idea how to do it!"

"Oh, that is no problem," replied the strange little man. "What will you give me if I do it for you?"

The miller's daughter stared at him in astonishment. "I . . . I will give you my necklace!" she replied.

"Very well," said the little man and he accepted the necklace. Then he sat down at the spinning wheel and quickly set it whirring. Round and round it turned. Soon the bobbin was full of gold thread. Then the little man put another bobbin on the spinning wheel. Soon that one was full, too. And on he

went all night long until he had spun all the straw
into shining gold thread!

The miller's daughter was overjoyed, and she
thanked the little man with all her heart. Then, as
the sun rose over the horizon, the strange little man
vanished.

Soon the
king came to see if
the miller's daughter had
spun the straw into gold. When he
saw all the gold thread, he was amazed
and delighted. Yet the sight of so much gold only
made the king greedier. So he led the miller's
daughter to another room.

This room was larger than the first and also filled
with straw. "You must spin all this straw into gold by
morning," the king told the miller's daughter, "or you
will lose your life."

As soon as the king had gone and locked the door behind him, the miller's daughter burst into tears.

Then the door slowly opened, and in walked the same strange little man.

"Good day, miller's daughter," he said. "What will you give me if I spin the straw into gold for you this time?"

"I . . . I will give you my ring!" she replied.

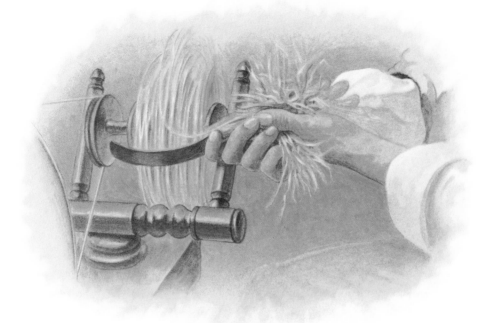

So the strange little man accepted the ring from the young woman's finger. Then he sat down at the spinning wheel and began spinning the straw into gold. And as soon as he was finished he disappeared.

Soon after dawn, the king came to see if the miller's daughter had completed her task. His eyes grew wide at the brilliance of the gold. But it only made him want to have more. So he led the miller's daughter to a third room.

This room was even larger, and it was piled to the ceiling with straw.

"You must spin all this straw into gold before the sun rises tomorrow," the king told the miller's daughter. "If you fail, you will lose your life. But if you succeed I will marry you and make you my wife." The king was thinking to himself that though she was only a miller's daughter, he would never find a richer wife anywhere.

After the king had left the miller's daughter and locked the door behind him, the strange little man once again appeared.

"What will you give me this time for spinning all this straw into gold?" he asked the miller's daughter.

The girl began to sob. "I have nothing left to give you," she answered.

"It is all right," said the little man. "Just promise me this: that when you are queen, you will give me your first child."

The miller's daughter hesitated. Then she gave the strange little man her promise. "Who knows if I shall ever be queen," she thought. "Besides, if I do not agree, then I will surely lose my life tomorrow."

So the little man sat down at the spinning wheel and set it turning. On and on it whirred until all the straw in the room had been spun into shining gold.

The next morning the king came in and saw the immense gold treasure shimmering like the light of a thousand suns. He married the miller's beautiful daughter that very day. She was now a queen with fine robes and a crown on her head.

Within a year, the queen gave birth to a beautiful baby boy. She was overjoyed to have a child of her own. In her happiness, she forgot her promise to the strange little man.

One day, as the queen was playing with her baby son, the little man visited her.

"I have come to claim what you promised me," he said, stretching out his arms toward the child.

The queen was horrified. "Please do not take my little son," she pleaded. "I will give you anything— anything you wish. Only leave me my son!"

Then she offered the strange little man all the wealth and riches in the kingdom, if he would only spare her child.

At first, the little man refused. But the queen began to weep so sorrowfully that he took pity on her. "Very well," he said. "I will give you three days to guess my name. If you do so in that time, you may keep your little son. But if you fail, the child must be mine." And with that the strange little man vanished.

The queen stayed awake all night. She thought of every name she had ever heard. Then she took her candle and went to the palace library and searched through all the books for strange and unusual names.

The next morning when the little man appeared, the queen began asking him, "Is your name Peter? Is your name John? Is your name Charlemagne?"

Each time the little man replied, "Oh, no! That is not my name!"

Then the queen recited all the names she knew one after the other. But to each one the little man replied,

"Oh, no! That is not my name!" Finally, she could think of no more names and the little man went away.

The queen summoned to her all the learned men of the king-dom and asked them to tell her all the strange and unusual names they had ever heard. She sent out her servants far and wide to collect as many odd names as they could.

When the little man came the next day, she asked him, "Is your name Big-Boots? Is your name Turtle-Beak? Can your name be Mutton-Chop or Crooked-Knees?"

But to each name the little man replied as before, "Oh, no! That is not my name!"

The queen did not know what to do.

On the third day, one of the queen's servants came to her and told a curious story.

"I searched far and wide, but I could not find a single new name," the man began. "Then on my way back through the mountains I came upon a tiny cottage. A fire was blazing in front of it, and a little man was dancing around the fire on one foot. As he danced, he sang this song:

I'll rest tomorrow and bake today
Then I'll take the queen's son away.
For no one will ever guess who I am
And that Rumpelstiltskin is my name!

The queen clapped her hands for joy.

When the little man came the next morning, she asked him, "Is your name Henry?"

"No!" he replied.

"Is your name Roland?"

"No!"

"Then can your name be . . . Rumpelstiltskin?"

The little man's mouth fell open. "Who told you that? Who told you that?" he shrieked.

And he became so cross, he tugged at his little beard and stamped his foot. He stamped so hard that the ground cracked open beneath him and swallowed him up! And that was the last anyone ever saw of Rumpelstiltskin!

THE LITTLE MATCH GIRL

By HANS CHRISTIAN ANDERSEN

Retold by SAMANTHA EASTON

Illustrated by ERIN AUGENSTINE

It was the last night of the year, and it was a very cold, dark night. The streets were empty. Everyone was home in their warm houses, busily cooking their New Year's Eve feast of roast goose and chestnut stuffing and apple pie and other good things.

Though it was very late, a little girl could be seen still walking slowly down the icy streets.

She had no hat on her head nor any shoes on her feet. When she left her house that morning, she had been wearing a pair of old slippers that were full of holes. They were far too big for her, and they had fallen off as she ran across the street to get out of the way of an oncoming carriage. One of them had vanished altogether, and a little boy had run off with the other one, saying it was so large, it would make a fine boat for his tin soldiers.

Since then, the little girl had had to go barefoot, and her little feet were blue with cold.

In her ragged apron, the little girl carried matches, and she held a packet of them in her hand. She was supposed to be selling them, but no one had bought a single match from her all day or given her so much as a copper penny. Now, the child was shivering and faint with hunger as she walked forlornly through the darkness.

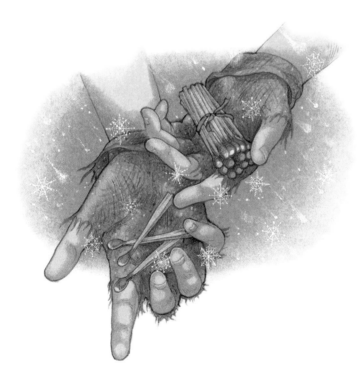

Sometimes, she stopped to stare into the lighted windows of the houses along the streets. All the houses were decorated in honor of the New Year. Delicious smells wafted out to the street, making the little girl feel hungrier.

At last, she came to a corner between two tall stone houses that was sheltered from the icy wind.

The little girl sat down there and pulled her feet under her, hoping to warm them. But it did no good. The cold air seemed to sink into her very bones.

The little girl was afraid to go home, for she had not sold any matches that day. She knew her father would probably beat her for that. Besides, it was not much warmer at home than it was outside in the street—the walls of their rooms were so full of holes.

Her mother had tried to stuff them with straw and rags, but the wind howled through them as strong as ever.

The little girl stretched out her hands. They were stiff with cold. "If I lit just one of these matches," she thought, "I would feel so much warmer!" She gazed longingly at the packet of matches in her hand.

Then she drew one out and struck it against the wall, making a loud scratch. The match sputtered and flared, casting a bright, clear light.

The little girl stared at it. All of a sudden, it seemed to her that she was sitting in front of a big iron stove with feet of brightly polished brass. Inside, a coal fire blazed brightly.

How warm and beautiful that fire was! Eagerly, the little girl stretched out her hands toward it. She pulled out her little bare feet to warm them by the glowing embers of the wonderful fire. But just then, the match went out.

The big iron stove vanished, and the little girl found herself on the cold, dark street again, holding a half-burned match in her hand.

The little girl pulled out another match and struck it. The flame rose, casting a light on the stone wall beside her. Suddenly the walls looked as transparent as glass.

It seemed to the child that she could see right through the wall into a room. There was a long table covered with a snow-white cloth and set with fine china, crystal glasses, and silver forks and knives and spoons. In the center, an enormous platter held a steaming roast goose stuffed with apples and sausage. How delicious it looked!

Then, something even more wonderful happened. The goose leaped off the platter, and with a knife and fork still stuck in its breast, came walking toward the little girl. She reached out her hands toward it. But as she did so the match went out.

Once again everything turned dark, and the little girl found herself staring only at the damp stone wall.

As quickly as she could, she pulled out another match and struck it.

This time the light blazed forth even more brightly, and the little girl found herself gazing up at an enormous Christmas tree.

It was much larger and more splendidly decorated than any Christmas tree she had ever seen. Even the ones she had glimpsed through the windows of rich people's houses could not compare with it.

Hundreds upon hundreds of lit candles gleamed in its green branches. Colored pictures of angels hung from it—pictures such as those the little girl had sometimes seen in shop windows at Christmastime. Only these pictures were even more lifelike and far more beautiful.

The child stretched out her hand toward the tree. Just then the match flickered out. But as the little girl watched, the candles on the Christmas tree seemed to rise higher and higher, until she realized she was staring at the stars in the sky.

They twinkled down at her so brightly and looked so beautiful she felt as if her heart would break. Then she saw one of them fall, leaving a bright trail of light behind it.

"Somebody must be dying," the little girl thought. Her grandmother, the one person in the world who had ever truly loved her, had once told her that whenever a star falls it means a soul is rising to heaven.

The little girl pulled out another match and struck it against the wall. This time, the light flared up in front of her, forming a bright circle like a halo.

In the center of it stood the little girl's grandmother. She looked so radiant and loving that the little girl could not help but cry out to her.

"Oh, Grandmother," she said. "Please take me with you. I know that when the match goes out you will vanish, just like the big warm stove and the lovely roast goose and the beautiful Christmas tree. Oh, Grandmother, please don't leave me here. Don't, please!"

And as the match burned out, the little girl desperately clutched the packet and struck the rest of the matches against the hard stone wall. They burst

into flame, and together they made a light that seemed brighter than the noonday sun.

In the blazing light, the little girl saw her grandmother again. The little girl stretched out her hands, and her grandmother gently took the child in her arms.

Then together they rose high above the dark icy streets to a place where there was no more hunger, no more cold, and no more pain or suffering. They rose all the way to heaven.

Early the next morning some passersby came upon the little match girl.

She was still sitting in the corner between the two houses, leaning against the wall. She was smiling but her small cheeks were pale, for she had frozen to death during the night. "Oh, the poor child," the people mourned.

Some of the people pointed at the bundle of burnt matches the child held in her hand. "Look!" they said. "The little creature must have tried to warm herself!"

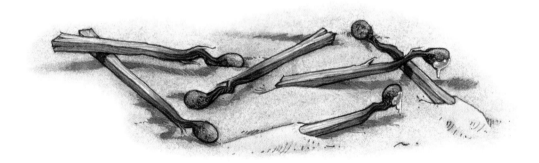

But they could not possibly know all the wonders the little match girl had seen that night. Nor would anyone know how joyfully she and her grandmother had celebrated the coming of the New Year.

THE THREE LITTLE PIGS

Retold by JENNIFER GREENWAY

Illustrated by DEBBIE DIENEMAN

*O*nce upon a time, there were three little pigs who lived in a broken-down cottage with their mother. As they were very poor, the three little pigs decided that it was none too early for them to go into the world and seek their fortunes. So the first little pig packed his favorite belongings, said good-bye to his mother, and set off.

He hadn't gone far before he came to a fine road paved with stones.

"What a beautiful road," said the first little pig. "I believe I will walk down it and see what I can find."

After a while the first little pig came upon a man carrying a big bundle of straw.

"Good morning, sir," said the first little pig. "Please sell me that bundle of straw so that I can make myself a house."

"Certainly," said the man.

So the first little pig gave the man all his money, and the man gave him the bundle of straw.

The first little pig got right to work. He lashed the straw to a coil. Then he wound the coil round and round to build up the walls. Soon the first little pig had made himself a cozy little house of straw, and he was very pleased.

But just as the first little pig was sitting down to his first supper in his new home, along came a big, bad wolf. The wolf had been hunting in the woods all day without finding anything to eat, and he was very hungry. When he saw the little pig's house, he thought, "Now I have found my supper!" The wolf knocked on the little pig's door and cried:

Little pig, little pig!
Let me in!

The first little pig peered out the window. When he saw the big, bad wolf, he said:

No, indeed, I won't let you in!
Not by the hair of my chinny-chin-chin!

That made the wolf cross. So he growled in a very loud voice:

Then I'll huff and I'll puff,
And I'll blow your house down!

But the first little pig still wouldn't let him in. So the big, bad wolf huffed and he puffed until the little house of straw came tumbling down. The first little pig had to run away as fast as he could, or the wolf would have surely eaten him up!

Shortly afterward, the second little pig decided it was time for him to seek his fortune. So he said good-bye to his mother and off he went.

He soon came to a road that was freshly paved with gravel. "What a nice, new road," thought the second little pig. "I believe I will walk down it and see what I can find."

So he turned onto the new gravel road.

Before long, the second little pig came upon a man carrying a big bundle of sticks.

"Good morning, sir," said the second little pig. "Please sell me that bundle of sticks so I can build myself a house."

"Certainly," said the man.

So the second little pig gave the man all his money. Then he took the bundle of sticks and got to work.

The second little pig sawed the sticks neatly. Then he nailed them together. Before long he had made himself a cozy little house of sticks.

But no sooner had the second little pig finished putting on the front door than along came the big, bad wolf.

The wolf knocked loudly at the door and cried:

Little pig, little pig!
Let me in!

When the second little pig peeked out of the window and saw the big, bad wolf, he replied:

No, indeed, I won't let you in!
Not by the hair of my chinny-chin-chin!

That made the wolf cross. So the wolf growled in a very loud voice:

Then I'll huff and I'll puff,
And I'll blow your house down!

The second little pig was frightened, but he still wouldn't let the wolf in.

So the big, bad wolf began to huff and puff.

He huffed and he puffed and he puffed and he huffed.

Before long, the big, bad wolf blew down the second little pig's house of sticks—right down to the ground.

The second little pig had to run away as fast as he could, or the big, bad wolf would have surely eaten him up!

After a while, the third little pig decided it was time for him to go into the world and seek his fortune.

So he packed his belongings and said good-bye to his mother. Then off he went.

After a while he came to a small dirt road. "What a quiet little road," the third little pig said to himself. "I believe I shall go down it and see what I can find."

So the third little pig walked down the dirt road.

Soon he came upon a man carrying a big load of bricks.

"Good morning, sir," said the third little pig. "Please sell me your load of bricks so I can build myself a house."

"Certainly," said the man.

So the third little pig gave the man all his money, and the man gave him the bricks.

The third little pig mixed up some cement, and he carefully laid the bricks one on top of the other. Before long, the little pig had built himself a cozy, sturdy little house of bricks.

No sooner had the third little pig gone inside than along came the big, bad wolf. The wolf knocked on the door as loudly as he could and cried:

Little pig, little pig!
Let me in!

But the third little pig had seen the big, bad wolf coming, and so he replied:

No, indeed, I won't let you in.
Not by the hair of my chinny-chin-chin!

The wolf was very cross when he heard that! So he growled in a big voice:

Then I'll huff and I'll puff
And I'll blow your house down!

Then the wolf huffed and puffed. And he puffed and he huffed. And he huffed and he puffed some more. But no matter how hard he tried, he could not blow down the little house of bricks! So the wolf climbed onto the roof and stuck his head down the chimney.

"I am just poking my nose inside," he said.

"As you like," said the third little pig.

"Now I am just putting my ears inside," said the wolf.

"Fine with me," said the third little pig.

"Now I am just putting my paws inside," said the wolf.

"Very well," said the third little pig.

"Now I am just putting my tail inside," said the wolf. And he fell down the third little pig's chimney!

Suddenly, the wolf gave a terrible howl, for the clever little pig had set a big kettle of water to boil in the fireplace!

The big, bad wolf had to scramble back up the chimney as fast as he could, for otherwise, he surely would have been boiled alive in the third little pig's big kettle.

And so the big, bad wolf ran away, and the third little pig lived happily ever after in his cozy, sturdy little house of bricks!

LITTLE RED RIDING HOOD

By THE BROTHERS GRIMM

Retold by JENNIFER GREENWAY

Illustrated by ELIZABETH MILES

There once lived a girl whose name was Little Red Riding Hood. She was called that because she always wore a red velvet cloak and hood that her grandmother had made for her.

Now her grandmother had been feeling ill, and one day Little Red Riding Hood's mother said to her, "I want you to take this basket of cakes and honey to Granny."

"Now go straight to Granny's," her mother told her, "and be sure you don't speak to any strangers on the way, and whatever you do, don't stray from the path!" Little Red Riding Hood promised to do as she was told.

Her grandmother lived on the other side of a great forest. So, Little Red Riding Hood went skipping quickly down the path with her basket under her arm.

She had not gone far when she met a big wolf.

"Good morning, Little Red Riding Hood," said the wolf. "Where are you going in such a hurry?"

Little Red Riding Hood did not know what a wicked creature the wolf was, so she replied politely, "I am going to see my grandmother. She has been ill, and I am bringing her this basket of cakes and honey."

"How nice," said the wolf. But to himself he thought, "What good luck! If I am clever I can have both Little Red Riding Hood and her grandmother for supper!"

Then he smiled at Little Red Riding Hood and said, "How lovely the woods look today! What a pity you have to rush on such a beautiful morning!"

Little Red Riding Hood looked around. Sunbeams were dancing in the trees, and bright flowers were waving their heads in the breeze. "I'm sure Grandmother would love a bouquet of flowers," she thought. "It's so early that surely I can stop for just a few minutes and pick some."

So Little Red Riding Hood left the path and skipped into the woods to pick flowers. Meanwhile the wolf ran as fast as he could to Grandmother's house.

When the wolf reached Grandmother's house, he knocked on the door.

"Who's there?" called Little Red Riding Hood's grandmother.

"It is I, Little Red Riding Hood!" said the wolf, disguising his voice. "I've brought you a basket of cakes and honey."

"I am too sick to get out of bed," Grandmother replied. "But the door is open, Little Red Riding Hood, just let yourself in and come up to my bedroom."

So the wicked wolf pushed open the door, came inside and climbed the stairs to Grandmother's bedroom. Then he went to Grandmother's bed and gobbled up the old woman!

Then the wicked wolf pulled one of Grandmother's flannel nightgowns over his head, even though it was much too small for him. Next, he put on Grandmother's warm woolen dressing gown. He even took Grandmother's spectacles and stuck them on the end of his long nose.

Then the wolf looked at himself in the mirror. He didn't look anything like Grandmother. And his long ears were showing. So the wolf put on Grandmother's lace nightcap, to try to hide them.

Then he climbed into Grandmother's bed, drew the covers over his nose, and settled back to wait for Little Red Riding Hood.

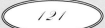

Meanwhile Little Red Riding Hood was still in the woods picking flowers. Every time she picked one, she seemed to see a prettier one just a little ways off. And so she strayed farther and farther from the path.

When she had picked so many flowers that she could not hold even one more, she returned to the path and headed again for Grandmother's house.

When Little Red Riding Hood arrived, she was surprised to find the door open.

"Hello," she called. "Grandmother, it's me."

"Just come in!" came Grandmother's voice. "I am too ill to get out of bed!"

How strange her grandmother's voice sounded. "She must be very ill," thought Little Red Riding Hood. So the little girl ran up the stairs to her grandmother's bedroom.

Little Red Riding Hood stood beside her grandmother's bed. How strange her grandmother looked!

"Why, Grandmother," she said. "What big ears you have!"

"All the better to hear you with, my dear," said the wolf.

"But, Grandmother, what big eyes you have!" said Little Red Riding Hood.

"All the better to see you with, my dear," said the wolf.

"But, Grandmother, what big hands you have!" said Little Red Riding Hood.

"All the better to hug you with, my dear," said the wolf.

"But, Grandmother," said Little Red Riding Hood. "What big teeth you have!"

"All the better to eat you with, my dear," said the wolf.

And with that the wicked wolf jumped out of the bed and opened his jaws wide.

"Why, you're not Grandmother!" cried Little Red Riding Hood.

"No, I'm not," said the wolf. "And I'm going to eat you up!"

Then the wolf snapped at Little Red Riding Hood and swallowed her in a single gulp!

After that, the wolf felt full. He rubbed his belly contentedly. "That was a good meal," he said, and then he started to yawn. "Now I could do with a nap!"

So the wolf climbed back into Grandmother's bed. Then he pulled the covers over his head and closed his eyes.

Soon the wolf was fast asleep and he began to snore very loudly. He snored so loudly that all the windows in Grandmother's house rattled.

Toward evening, a huntsman came walking by and heard the wolf snoring.

"That is strange," he thought to himself. "The old woman is snoring awfully loudly! I wonder if she is all right."

So the huntsman walked up to Grandmother's house. To his great surprise the door was wide open. "Hello! Hello!" called the huntsman. "Is anybody home?"

But there was no answer. The wicked wolf was sleeping too soundly to hear the huntsman.

"I'll just go in and make sure everything is all right," the huntsman thought. So he went inside and tiptoed up the stairs.

As he climbed the stairs, the snoring grew louder and louder. The huntsman followed the snoring all the way to Grandmother's bed.

The huntsman looked at Grandmother's bed and saw the wolf lying fast asleep.

"Ah-ha," said the huntsman. "So it's you who is snoring so loudly, you rascal! I've been hunting for you for a long time, and now it looks as if I've got you!"

The huntsman raised his gun and was about to shoot the wolf when it occurred to him that the wolf might have eaten the old woman.

So the huntsman took a knife and cut open the wolf. Out stepped Little Red Riding Hood and her grandmother. They were both happy to be saved.

Then the huntsman filled the wolf's stomach with heavy stones and sewed it up. When the wolf awoke and saw the huntsman, he tried to run away. But the stones were so heavy that he fell down dead!

Then the huntsman, Little Red Riding Hood, and Grandmother ate all the delicious cakes and honey that Little Red Riding Hood had brought.

Soon Grandmother was feeling well again, and Little Red Riding Hood started home.

When she returned, Little Red Riding Hood told her mother everything that had happened. "Never again will I speak to strangers or stray from the path when you have told me not to!" she said.

Her mother hugged her tight. "I'm sure you won't," she said, and Little Red Riding Hood never did!

JACK *and the* BEANSTALK

Retold by JENNIFER GREENWAY

Illustrated by RICHARD BERNAL

Once upon a time there was a widow who lived in a tumbledown cottage with her son Jack. Jack and his mother were so poor that all they had was an old white cow.

One day when there was no food in the house, and no money to buy any, the widow said to herself, "I will have to sell our cow, or Jack and I will surely starve."

So Jack's mother called him to her and said, "I want you to take the cow to market and sell her. But be sure you get a good price, for she is all we have."

"Yes, Mother," Jack replied, and he put a collar on the cow and headed to town.

Jack was delighted to be going to market by himself. As he walked he whistled a cheerful tune.

He was interrupted when he heard someone say, "You seem to be in a fine mood, young man. Where are you going today?"

Jack turned around. On the side of the road stood a strange little man. He was about four feet tall and dressed in a bright green suit.

"Why, I'm off to market," Jack said, "to sell our old cow."

"I'll buy your cow, if you'd like," said the little man.

"What will you give me for her?" asked Jack.

"I'll give you these magic beans," the little man replied. Then he opened his hand. Jack looked at the beans in the man's palm. They were all the colors of the rainbow.

"Magic beans!" Jack cried. "I've never seen any before!" And he traded the cow for the beautiful magic beans.

"Mother will be so happy," Jack thought, feeling very pleased with himself. Then he ran home as fast as he could to show her the magic beans.

But Jack's mother was not happy when she learned what he had done.

"Oh, Jack," she cried. "How could you be so stupid! You traded our cow for a handful of beans!" Jack's mother was so angry, she picked up the magic beans and threw them out the window.

Jack realized his mistake, but it was too late. The cow was gone and there was still nothing to eat for supper. Jack went to bed, feeling very foolish.

All night, Jack tossed and turned. "My poor mother and I will have nothing to eat tomorrow either," he thought miserably. "And it is all because of me and those magic beans!"

The next morning, Jack gloomily climbed out of bed. When he went to the window, he saw an amazing sight.

Where his mother had thrown the magic beans, a giant beanstalk was growing. It was thick and tall—so tall that it reached into the clouds!

"Mother, come quickly!" Jack called. And together they stood in the garden, staring in wonder at the beanstalk.

"I wonder where it goes," Jack said. "Perhaps I'll climb it and find out!"

"You'll do no such thing," said his mother. "Those beans have already caused enough trouble!"

But it was too late, for Jack had already started up the beanstalk. Up he climbed, higher and higher, until the cottage below looked no bigger than a bird's nest. Still, Jack could not see to the top of the beanstalk.

At last, Jack climbed through the clouds. There he found himself at the top of the beanstalk. A field of clouds stretched in every direction. In the distance, Jack could see an enormous stone castle.

He jumped off the beanstalk and walked toward the castle. Soon he stood before the entrance—a huge iron door. Not knowing what else to do, Jack pulled the bell. After a moment, the great door slowly swung open.

To Jack's horror, there stood a huge, ugly giantess looking down at him. Before Jack could run away, the giantess scooped him up in her huge hand. "Oh, good!" she said in a great big voice. "I've been looking for someone to help me with my chores."

Jack was so frightened, all he could say was, "Of course. What do you want me to do?"

"Well," said the giantess. "First you may help me light the fire and polish the boots. Now, we must be very careful when my husband comes home, for there is nothing he likes better than to eat roasted Englishmen for dinner!"

Jack didn't like the sound of that. But the giantess promised that she would hide Jack in the cupboard when her husband came. So he helped her light the fire and polish her boots.

All of a sudden, Jack heard a terrible sound like the roaring of thunder.

"That's my husband," the giantess cried, and she quickly hid Jack in the cupboard. Then Jack heard a great booming voice:

Fe, fi, fo, fum!
I smell the blood of an Englishman.
Be he alive or be he dead
I'll grind his bones to make my bread!

And in stomped the giant.

He was much bigger than his wife and much uglier, too. He sat down at the table and shouted, "I smell an Englishman. Catch him and roast him at once!"

"Don't be silly," replied his wife. "That's only the mutton stew I've cooked for your supper." Peering through the keyhole of the cupboard, Jack watched her set down the biggest bowl of mutton stew he had ever seen.

The bowl of stew was so big that Jack could have sailed one of his small boats across it. The giant quickly ate the stew. He called for another bowl, and ate that too.

When he was finished, the giant said to his wife, "Now bring me the goose that lays the golden eggs." His wife brought a very ordinary-looking goose and set it before the giant. Then she went to bed.

After she was gone, the giant turned to the goose and said, "Lay!" The goose promptly laid an egg of pure gold. "Lay!" the giant said a second time, and the goose laid another golden egg. "Lay!" the giant commanded a third time, and the goose laid a third egg of gold.

Jack's eyes grew wide as he watched through the keyhole. "A goose that lays golden eggs!" he thought to himself. "Why, that would be a fine thing to have!" Jack wondered how he might steal it.

After a time, the giant's eyelids began to grow heavy and soon he fell asleep right at the table. He snored so loudly that the walls of the castle shook.

When Jack was quite sure that the giant was fast asleep, he crept out of the cupboard and tiptoed across the table. Then he snatched the goose that laid the golden eggs.

With the magic goose under his arm, Jack leaped off the table and ran across the stone floor toward the door. Just as he reached it, however, the terrified goose cried, "Help! I'm being stolen. Help!"

The giant awoke with a start. When he spotted Jack with the goose, he came racing after them!

"Stop," the giant shouted. "Stop, thief! Give me back my goose!"

But Jack didn't stop. He was too frightened to turn around. He kept running as fast as he could across the clouds to the giant beanstalk.

At last, he saw the top of the beanstalk. And still clutching the magic goose, he started climbing down the beanstalk. But he had not gone far, when the beanstalk began to sway violently.

Looking up, Jack saw that the giant was coming down the beanstalk after him! Jack began to climb down faster. The giant began climbing down faster, too. Just as the giant was about to catch up with him, Jack reached the bottom of the beanstalk.

He saw his mother standing by the cottage door, and he called to her, "Mother, quick! Fetch me the axe!"

His mother came running with the axe. Jack grabbed it and, with a single blow, chopped through the beanstalk.

With a great groan, the beanstalk came crashing down, and the giant fell with it. Now, where the giant landed no one knows, but Jack and his mother never saw him again.

Jack showed his mother the goose that laid the golden eggs, and she fed it some dried corn. The goose was so happy to be free from the giant that it laid a golden egg, then another, and another. Jack took the golden eggs to market and traded them for food and a new cow and much more besides.

And ever after Jack had climbed that giant beanstalk, he and his mother and the goose that laid the golden eggs all lived happily together.

$\mathscr{S}$LEEPING $\mathscr{B}$EAUTY

Retold by SAMANTHA EASTON

Illustrated by LYNN BYWATERS

Once upon a time there lived a king and queen who longed to have a child. After many years their wish came true, and the queen gave birth to a beautiful baby girl.

The king was beside himself with joy, and he planned a splendid feast in honor of his newborn daughter. He invited all his relatives and all the great lords and ladies of the kingdom.

The king also invited the magic fairies who lived in the kingdom. He hoped they would give his child their blessing.

Now there were thirteen fairies in the kingdom, but only twelve received invitations to the feast. Somehow the king forgot to send an invitation to the thirteenth.

The twelve fairies came to the great celebration, and each presented her magical gift to the king's daughter. The first fairy gave the child beauty, the second a kind heart, the third a quick wit, the fourth charm. And on it went, until the king's daughter had received every delightful talent and trait.

But after the eleventh fairy had given her gift, the thirteenth fairy stormed into the hall. She was furious that she had not been invited to the feast. Without a word of greeting, she turned to the king and shouted in a harsh voice, "I, too, have come to give the princess a gift. On her fifteenth birthday, your daughter will prick herself on a spindle and fall dead!"

And at that the thirteenth fairy turned and strode out of the palace.

The queen began to cry and the king turned pale. But then the twelfth fairy stepped forward.

"I have not given the princess my gift yet," the twelfth fairy said, "and while I cannot undo the curse, I can soften it. Your daughter will not die when she pricks her finger. Instead, she will fall into a deep sleep that will last for one hundred years."

The king, who wished to save his beloved daughter from this fate, immediately ordered all the spinning wheels and spindles in the kingdom to be burned at once.

Years passed and the little princess grew. As the fairies had promised she was beautiful and kind and clever, and each year she grew more charming and lovely. Everyone who knew her loved her and she passed her days happily in the kingdom.

On the day of the princess's fifteenth birthday, her parents' presence was requested by a neighboring king. So they left the princess behind in the castle. "Now you must behave yourself while we are gone," her mother told her.

"Of course," the princess promised.

But the princess had never been without her parents before and she was delighted. "I will be able to wander about the castle as I please," she thought, "and look at everything."

All that day the princess amused herself exploring the castle. She followed every unused corridor she could find and peered into forgotten dusty rooms.

At last, she found herself at the foot of a small winding staircase. She climbed the stairs until she came to an old wooden door with a rusty key in the lock. The princess turned the key and slowly pushed the door open.

Inside, a very, very old woman sat before a spinning wheel. The princess had never seen a spinning wheel and was very curious about it. The old woman was busily spinning thread onto the spindle. The wheel whirred around so merrily that the princess could not help exclaiming, "How wonderful! What is this, Grandmother? What are you doing?"

"Ah," the old woman replied. "This is a spinning wheel and this is a spindle and I am spinning thread."

The princess watched in admiration as the spindle filled with bright thread. "May I please try?" she asked.

Then she reached for the twirling spindle, and in her eagerness she pricked her finger.

"Oh!" she cried, letting go of the spindle. She suddenly felt very sleepy, and for a moment she was sure the old woman was laughing at her.

"Dear me, Grandmother," the princess cried. "I feel so strange! Let me lie down on that bed in the corner." Within moments she had fallen into a deep, deep sleep.

This sleep seemed to creep softly and silently through the castle like a quiet mist. The king and queen, who had just returned, began to yawn. Then slowly closing their eyes, they too slept. The same thing happened to their courtiers and footmen and ladies-in-waiting, until the whole court had fallen asleep where they stood.

The guards at the palace gate let their swords slide from their hands as they slipped into a deep sleep. The palace dogs and cats curled up and closed their eyes. The horses slumbered in their stables. The birds on the rooftop stopped chirping and tucked their heads under their wings. Even the flies stopped buzzing and lay still.

In the kitchen, the cook fell asleep just as she was reaching out to box the scullery boy's ears. He fell asleep, too. So did the kitchen maid, who was sitting at the fire basting some chickens on a spit.

Even the fire in the hearth stopped its crackling and died away. The wind outside stopped blowing. Soon the entire castle was quiet and covered with a blanket of sleep.

Then thick, thorny vines sprang up around the castle. They grew and grew, higher and higher each day, until nothing could be seen of the castle any-more—not its golden gates or its high stone walls or the tops of its golden towers or even the bright flags that flew from them.

Finally the castle was completely covered by a thick screen of thorns.

Across the land people spoke in whispers of the castle hidden behind the thorns. They whispered of the princess who lay inside the palace in a deep enchanted sleep, and they called her the Sleeping Beauty.

Soon princes from far and wide came to the castle. They longed to see Sleeping Beauty with their own

eyes and tried to break through the thick, thorny vines.

And while all these princes were brave and strong, none of them was able to reach the enchanted castle. Whenever they tried to hack through the thicket, the vines clung together so tightly that no sword could cut through them. Many a brave prince became trapped in the thorns and died.

Many years passed. One day, a handsome young prince came riding through the country near the kingdom. He happened to hear an old man telling the story of the enchanted castle hidden behind the thorns. When the old man spoke of Sleeping Beauty, the prince felt a great longing to see her.

"Where is this castle?" he asked the old man. "Please tell me how I might find it!"

The old man begged him not to go there. "I can see that you are brave," he told the prince. "But many a king's son as brave and fair as you has died trying to glimpse the Sleeping Beauty."

Then he told the prince how the great thorny vines closed so tightly around all who tried to pass that they could not escape.

"I am not afraid," the prince replied. "I must see Sleeping Beauty!"

So the old man sighed and told him the way to the castle.

When the prince found the castle, the hundred years were just ending. The day had come when Sleeping Beauty was to awaken.

As the prince approached the thicket, beautiful roses suddenly bloomed on its branches. Then the branches parted to let him pass.

The prince rode through the castle gates, across
the sleeping courtyard, and up to the palace. Leaving
his horse, he walked through the throne room and
past the sleeping king and queen. In every hall and
room he entered, not one living thing stirred. The
castle was so quiet that the beating of the prince's
heart sounded as loud to him as the beating of a
drum.

At last, he came to a small spiral staircase. Upon
climbing it, he found a small wooden door. He

pushed the door open and gasped. There lay Sleeping Beauty. She lay on the bed as fast asleep as she had been for a hundred years. She was so beautiful that the prince could not help bending over to kiss her.

At his kiss, Sleeping Beauty opened her eyes. The prince smiled at her. She gazed deep into his eyes. It seemed to her that somehow she already knew him, for he was the one she had been waiting for all these years. Then the prince took her hand, and together they went down into the castle.

As they walked, the castle sprang to life again. The horses in the courtyard neighed, the dogs barked, the cats purred, and the birds ruffled their feathers and chirped.

The guards sprang to their feet and picked up their swords. And in the kitchen, the cook boxed the scullery boy's ears. The kitchen maid started turning the chickens on the spit, while the fire crackled to life.

The king and queen opened their eyes and looked around in surprise, as did their courtiers and footmen and ladies-in-waiting. The prince asked Sleeping Beauty to be his wife, and she said yes. Their wedding was celebrated that very day, and a more joyous wedding has never been seen. And ever after that the Sleeping Beauty and her prince lived very happily.

THE TALE of PETER RABBIT

By BEATRIX POTTER

Illustrated by ROBYN OFFICER

Once upon a time there were four little Rabbits, and their names were—Flopsy, Mopsy, Cotton-tail, . . . and Peter.

They lived with their mother in a sandbank, underneath the root of a very big fir-tree.

"Now, my dears," said old Mrs. Rabbit one morning, "you may go into the fields or down the lane, but don't go into Mr. McGregor's garden: your father had an accident there; he was put in a pie by Mrs. McGregor.

"Now run along, and don't get into mischief. I am going out."

Then old Mrs. Rabbit took a basket and her umbrella, and went through the wood to the baker's. She bought a loaf of brown bread and five currant buns.

Flopsy, Mopsy, and Cotton-tail, who were good little bunnies, went down the lane to gather blackberries:

But Peter, who was very naughty, ran straight away to Mr. McGregor's garden, and squeezed under the gate!

First he ate some lettuces and some French beans; and then he ate some radishes;

And then, feeling rather sick, he went to look for some parsley.

But round the end of a cucumber frame, whom should he meet but Mr. McGregor!

Mr. McGregor was on his hands and knees planting out young cabbages, but he jumped up and ran after Peter, waving a rake and calling out, "Stop thief!"

Peter was most dreadfully frightened; he rushed all over the garden, for he had forgotten the way back to the gate.

He lost one of his shoes among the cabbages, and the other shoe amongst the potatoes.

After losing them, he ran on four legs and went faster, so that I think he might have got away altogether if he had not unfortunately run into a gooseberry net, and got caught by the large buttons on his jacket. It was a blue jacket with brass buttons, quite new.

Peter gave himself up for lost, and shed big tears; but his sobs were overheard by some friendly sparrows, who flew to him in great excitement, and implored him to exert himself.

Mr. McGregor came up with a sieve, which he intended to pop upon the top of Peter; but Peter wriggled out just in time, leaving his jacket behind him.

And rushed into the toolshed, and jumped into a can. It would have been a beautiful thing to hide in, if it had not had so much water in it.

Mr. McGregor was quite sure that Peter was somewhere in the toolshed, perhaps hidden underneath a flowerpot. He began to turn them over carefully, looking under each.

Presently Peter sneezed—"Kerty-schoo!" Mr. McGregor was after him in no time.

And tried to put his foot upon Peter, who jumped out of a window, upsetting three plants. The window was too small for Mr. McGregor, and he was tired of running after Peter. He went back to his work.

Peter sat down to rest; he was out of breath and trembling with fright, and he had not the least idea which way to go. Also he was very damp with sitting in that can.

After a time he began to wander about, going lippity—lippity—not very fast, and looking all round.

He found a door in a wall; but it was locked, and there was no room for a fat little rabbit to squeeze underneath.

An old mouse was running in and out over the stone doorstep, carrying peas and beans to her family in the wood. Peter asked her the way to the gate, but she had such a large pea in her mouth that she could not answer. She only shook her head at him. Peter began to cry.

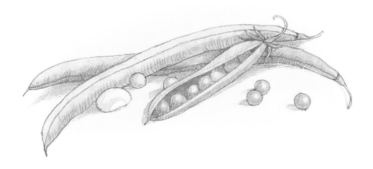

Then he tried to find his way straight across the garden, but he became more and more puzzled. Presently, he came to a pond where Mr. McGregor filled his water-cans. A white cat was staring at some goldfish, she sat very, very still, but now and then the tip of her tail twitched as if it were alive. Peter thought it best to go away without speaking to her; he had heard about cats from his cousin, little Benjamin Bunny.

He went back toward the toolshed, but suddenly, quite close to him, he heard the noise of a hoe—scr-r-ritch, scratch, scratch, scritch. Peter scuttered underneath the bushes. But presently, as nothing happened, he came out, and climbed upon a wheelbarrow and peeped over.

The first thing he saw was Mr. McGregor hoeing onions. His back was turned toward Peter, and beyond him was the gate!

Peter got down very quietly off the wheelbarrow and started running as fast as he could go, along a straight walk behind some black-currant bushes.

Mr. McGregor caught sight of him at the corner, but Peter did not care. He slipped underneath the gate, and was safe at last in the wood outside the garden.

Mr. McGregor hung up the little jacket and the shoes for a scarecrow to frighten the blackbirds.

Peter never stopped running or looked behind him till he got home to the big fir-tree.

He was so tired that he flopped down upon the nice soft sand on the floor of the rabbit-hole and shut his eyes. His mother was busy cooking; she wondered what he had done with his clothes. It was the second little jacket and pair of shoes that Peter had lost in a fortnight!

I am sorry to say that Peter was not very well during the evening.

His mother put him to bed, and made some chamomile tea; and she gave a dose of it to Peter!

"One tablespoonful to be taken at bedtime."

But Flopsy, Mopsy, and Cotton-tail had bread and milk and blackberries for supper.

The Steadfast Tin Soldier

By HANS CHRISTIAN ANDERSEN

Retold by SAMANTHA EASTON

Illustrated by MICHAEL MONTGOMERY

Once upon a time there were twenty-five toy tin soldiers. They were brothers, for they had all been made from the same tin spoon. They wore fine red and blue uniforms and carried little guns, and they all lived together in a carved wooden box.

The first words they ever heard came from a little boy as he lifted the lid off their wooden box. "Oh look!" the boy cried. "Tin soldiers!"

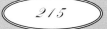

It was the boy's birthday and he had been given the tin soldiers as a present. Clapping his hands with delight, the boy set the tin soldiers on the table. They were all exactly alike except for one who had but one leg. He had been made last and there had not been enough tin left to finish him properly.

Besides the soldiers, the table was covered with all sorts of wonderful toys. The prettiest was a paper castle.

This castle was so beautifully made that through its windows could be seen little rooms complete with tiny paper furniture and tapestries. In front of the castle little paper trees stood around a small mirror that was meant to be a lake. And on the mirror lake swam tiny wax swans. All this was very lovely, but the loveliest part of the castle was a tiny dancer who stood in the castle door.

The dancer, too, was made of paper. She wore a dress of white tulle. A little blue ribbon was wrapped like a shawl around her shoulders. This ribbon was held in place with a silver sequin the same size as her face.

The little dancer's arms gracefully stretched out in front of her, and one of her legs was raised so high behind her that the little tin soldier could not see it.

"She must have only leg, just as I do!" he thought. "How pretty she is! She would make me the perfect wife!" Then he thought sadly, "But she is far too grand for me. She lives in a fine castle, while I live in a wooden box that I share with my brothers. Still, I must try to get to know her!"

So the little tin soldier stretched out on the table behind a snuffbox. From there he could watch the little dancer.

When evening came, the little boy put all the other tin soldiers back in their wooden box. Then the people of the house turned out the lights and went to bed.

When the people were asleep, the toys came to life and began to amuse themselves. They visited with each other and danced and played all sorts of games. The dolls waltzed. The teddy bears played leapfrog. The colored pencils chased each other over the drawing pad. And the cuckoo in the clock sang a lively song.

The tin soldiers rattled the lid of their box for they wished to get out and join the fun. Only the tin soldier and the little dancer stayed still. She stood on tiptoe in the castle door and held one leg stretched out behind her as steadily as the tin soldier stood on his one leg. The little tin soldier stared at the little dancer and she stared back, but neither of them spoke.

At the stroke of midnight, the lid of the snuffbox sprang open, and out popped a little red goblin.

"Tin soldier," growled the goblin. "You will please remember to keep your eyes to yourself!"

But the tin soldier pretended not to hear. Then the goblin said in a nasty voice, "Very well. I'll take care of you tomorrow!" With that he disappeared into the snuffbox.

Early the next morning, the little boy came running into the room with his brother. They picked up the little tin soldier and set him on the windowsill. Now, I don't know whether it was the red goblin's doing or not, but just then a strong gust of wind blew the little tin soldier off the sill.

Down, down the tin soldier fell—three stories onto the street below. It was a terrible fall. He landed headfirst with his gun stuck between two

cobblestones and his leg in the air. The children and
the maid ran outside to look for him but they
couldn't find him anywhere.

That afternoon, it began to rain. It was a quick,
hard rain that filled the gutters. When it was over,
two boys came out to play. "Look!" one of them cried.
"There's a tin soldier. Let's make him a boat!" So they
made a boat out of an old newspaper. Then they set
the little tin soldier in the boat and sent him sailing
down the gutter.

How fast the little paper boat went! How deep the water seemed! The little tin soldier could not help being frightened. But he bravely stood as straight as he could and held tightly to his gun.

Suddenly the little paper boat was swept into a drain and down a dark tunnel.

"How black it is in here," thought the little tin soldier. "Where am I going, I wonder? It is all the goblin's fault! Oh, if only the little dancer were here with me. Then I would not care even if it were twice as dark!"

Just then a large water rat swam up to the boat. "Where is your passport?" he hissed at the tin soldier. "Give it to me at once!" The tin soldier did not reply but grasped his gun more tightly. So the water rat gnashed his teeth and howled, "Stop him! Stop him! He hasn't shown his passport!" But the little paper boat was soon carried away by the current.

Now the soldier could see a light ahead. As the boat drew closer to the light, he heard a terrible roaring sound. It was loud enough to strike fear into the bravest heart. You see, the tunnel emptied into a canal. The plunge would be as dangerous for the tin soldier as an enormous waterfall would be for you or me. The little tin soldier was terribly afraid, but he stood as straight as ever and shouldered his gun.

The paper boat tumbled down into the canal. It whirled round and round and filled with water. The tin soldier did not move a muscle. Instead he thought of the pretty little dancer whom he was sure he would never see again. Then he remembered the words of an old military song:

Farewell, soldier, true and brave,
Going toward your cold, dark grave!

Finally the paper boat dissolved in the water, and the little tin soldier sank.

Just then a large fish swam by and swallowed the tin soldier. How dark it was inside the fish's belly— even darker than in the tunnel. But the little tin soldier still stood straight and bravely shouldered his gun.

The fish darted this way and that until the tin soldier felt terribly shaken up. Then, after a time, the fish was still. Next a flash of lightning seemed to pass through the fish, and the little tin soldier found himself in daylight again.

"Why, look!" cried a voice. "Here is the tin soldier!"

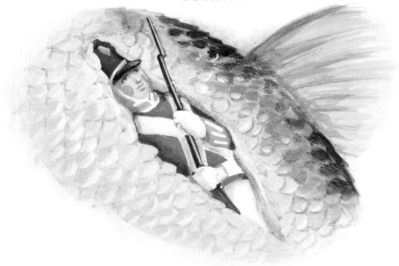

You see the fish had
been caught and taken to market where the cook had
bought him. She brought him back to the kitchen
and had cut him open with a big knife.

The cook picked up the tin soldier between her
fingers. Then she carefully carried him upstairs so
everyone could see the amazing little soldier who had
traveled so far in the belly of a fish.

When the cook set the tin soldier on the table, everyone cried in glee and admiration. The tin soldier looked around. To his amazement, he was back in the very room he had started from.

The little boy was there, and so were the other twenty-four tin soldiers, as well as all the rest of the toys. In the corner of the table stood the paper castle. The tin soldier saw that the pretty little dancer was still standing on one leg in the castle door, for she was as steadfast and true as he himself was.

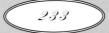

When the little tin soldier saw the dancer, he was so touched that if he could he would have wept tears of tin. But of course, he could not. So he only stared at the little dancer and she stared at him and neither of them spoke.

Just then the little boy picked up the tin soldier and threw him into the fire. I think this really must have been the red goblin's doing, for why else would the little boy have done such a thing?

Flames flared around the little tin soldier. The

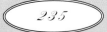

heat felt terrible to him, but whether it was the heat of the fire or the warmth of his feelings for the little dancer, he could not say. The bright colors faded from his uniform, but even that might have been from sorrow. He stared at the little dancer and she stared at him. He could feel himself melting away, but he still stood as straight as ever, for he was a brave, true soldier.

Just then the door of the room flew open and a draft of wind picked up the little dancer. She fluttered across the room right into the fire beside the little tin soldier.

Flames blazed around the little dancer and in a flash she was gone. Beside her the tin soldier slowly melted away into a lump of gray metal.

The next morning when the maid cleared away the ashes, all she found of the little tin soldier was a small tin heart. Of the pretty little dancer, nothing was left except her sequin, and that was burned as black as coal.

THUMBELINA

By HANS CHRISTIAN ANDERSEN

Retold by JENNIFER GREENWAY

Illustrated by ROBYN OFFICER

There once lived a couple who longed to have a child, but their wish did not come true. At last, the woman went to a fairy and asked for her help. The fairy gave her a seed and said, "Plant this in a flower-pot and water it carefully."

Soon a beautiful flower sprang up. It looked like a tulip with its petals tightly closed.

"How lovely," said the woman, kissing the flower. As she did so, the petals opened. Inside sat a tiny, graceful girl no bigger than the woman's thumb. The woman was overjoyed. She and her husband named the child Thumbelina.

Thumbelina's cradle was a walnut shell. She had a pillow of violets and a quilt of rose petals. At night her cradle sat on the windowsill. During the day, the woman kept a bowl filled with water on the table. Thumbelina amused herself by rowing around the bowl in a boat made of a large tulip petal. She used two white horsehairs for oars. As she rowed, she sang in the tiniest, prettiest voice imaginable.

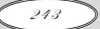

One night a big ugly toad hopped through the window. When the toad saw Thumbelina asleep in her cradle, she cried, "She would make the perfect wife for my son!"

The ugly toad snatched the cradle with Thumbelina inside and carried it to her home in the swamp.

The toad set Thumbelina on a large lily pad in the middle of the water so she could not escape. Then she went to fetch her son, who was even bigger and uglier than she was.

While the toad was gone, Thumbelina woke up. When she saw where she was, she began to cry and wonder how she would ever get home again. Some fish swimming below heard Thumbelina's cries.

When the fish saw how pretty Thumbelina was, they felt sorry for her. "We must set her free," they said, "so she does not have to marry the toad's son." The little fish began to bite at the stem of the lily

pad. Before long, they had gnawed through it, and the lily pad floated away.

Just then the toad returned with her son. "Stop!" the son called after Thumbelina. "Where are you going? You are to be my wife and live with me here in the swamp!" But it was too late. Thumbelina was already floating downstream.

Thumbelina went a long way, past wide green fields and deep shady woods. Birds and butterflies stopped to say hello to her, and she felt very happy.

Suddenly, a big brown beetle swooped down and seized Thumbelina in his claws. "How pretty you are!" he said. "I shall make you my wife!" How frightened Thumbelina was, but there was nothing she could do!

The beetle sat her on the branch of a tall tree to show her to the other beetles. But they did not think Thumbelina was pretty at all. "How ugly she is!" they sneered, turning up their feelers. "Her waist is so slim, and she has only two legs! She looks horrible!"

After that, the beetle decided he didn't want Thumbelina for a wife after all. So he flew her down from the tree and set her on a daisy.

Thumbelina was very sad, since she felt the beetles were right. She did not know that she was really very lovely.

All summer Thumbelina lived in the forest. She wove herself a bed of grass and hung it under a large leaf to shelter herself from the rain. She drank the morning dew and ate nectar from the flowers. She was perfectly content until autumn came—and then winter.

First, the leaf Thumbelina lived under died and
shriveled. Now she had no shelter from the wind and
rain. There was no longer any food to eat, either.
Then it began to snow, and Thumbelina almost froze
to death. So she went looking for food and shelter.

She walked until she came to a large cornfield.
The cornstalks had been cut long before. Nothing
was left but the stubble, which to Thumbelina
seemed as tall as a great forest. At last, she found the
home of a field mouse.

She knocked timidly on the door. When the field
mouse answered, Thumbelina said shyly, "Please, can
you spare a grain of barley?"

The field mouse, who was a kind thing, replied,
"Of course! Come in, you dear little creature!" She
led Thumbelina inside and fed her.

The field mouse's home was very comfortable, and her cupboards were full of the food she had stored for winter. So she told Thumbelina, "If you will keep my house tidy for me and tell me some good stories, you may stay with me all winter, if you like."

"Yes, please!" cried Thumbelina. And so she did all that the field mouse asked, and in return she was kept warm and well fed.

One day the field mouse said, "Listen, Thumbelina. My neighbor is coming to pay us a visit tomorrow. He is much richer than I, and he wears a beautiful black velvet coat. Oh, he is a very clever man! But he is blind, so be sure to tell him your very best stories."

"Of course," said Thumbelina. But she was not very excited about the visitor, for he was a mole.

The mole came the next day, wearing his black velvet coat. Even though he was very rich and probably very learned, as well, Thumbelina did not like him. He said dreadful things about the sun and the flowers and birds, yet he had never seen them.

Nevertheless, Thumbelina told him her best stories and sang him all the songs she knew. She had such a lovely voice that the mole fell in love with her. However, he did not say anything, because he was very cautious. Instead, he invited Thumbelina and the field mouse to pay him a visit.

So the three set out through a tunnel the mole had recently dug between his home and that of the field mouse. "Now, please watch your step," the mole told them. "It's quite dark here and there is a dead bird farther down the tunnel. But don't let that alarm you!"

When they came to the dead bird, the mole accidentally pushed his nose through the roof of the tunnel. The sun came shining through, and Thumbelina clearly saw the bird.

He was a swallow, and he did not look as if he had been dead for long. "Poor bird," Thumbelina thought sadly. "He must have died of the cold."

The mole pushed the bird aside roughly. "Useless creatures, birds!" he said gruffly. Thumbelina said nothing. But when the mole and the field mouse had gone ahead, she bent over and kissed the bird. "Perhaps you were one of the birds that sang to me all summer," she said. "How nice it was to hear your sweet music!"

After the mole showed them his house and gave them tea, he led them home again. Then he repaired the hole so no sunlight or cold could enter. But that night Thumbelina could not sleep.

She kept thinking of the poor swallow in the tunnel. At last, she crept from her bed and wove a blanket out of hay. She took it into the tunnel and laid it gently over the swallow.

Thumbelina sadly laid her head on the bird's breast. When she did, she heard a sound. It was the beating of the swallow's heart. He was not dead, only numb with cold. Thumbelina was afraid—the swallow was much bigger than she—but she bravely wrapped the blanket more tightly around him. Then she tiptoed away.

The next day she slipped away to visit the swallow again. He was awake now but very weak. So Thumbelina brought him water and honey, and all through the long cold winter she carefully nursed the swallow back to health. She told the field mouse and the mole nothing of this, for they did not think much of birds.

At last, spring came. The swallow was now well
enough to fly away. Thumbelina re-opened the hole
in the roof of the tunnel for him.

"Why don't you come with me?" the swallow
asked Thumbelina. "I can take you to warm, beautiful
places."

Thumbelina dearly wished she could go with the
swallow, but she shook her head. "The field mouse

has been very kind to me," she said, "I cannot just leave her!"

"Very well," said the swallow. "Farewell, kind maiden. I hope I see you again." And with that, the swallow flew away.

Tears filled Thumbelina's eyes. She was very fond of the swallow and would miss him so much.

Spring passed, then summer. Thumbelina worked for the field mouse, who treated her kindly but hardly ever let her go outside into the beautiful sunshine.

One day, as autumn was coming, the field mouse said to her, "I have good news, dear Thumbelina. The mole has asked for your hand in marriage. We must work to get your wedding clothes ready!"

"But I don't want to marry the mole!" cried Thumbelina, bursting into tears at the thought of living with him in his dark, underground tunnel far from the bright sun and all the lovely flowers.

"Don't be silly," the field mouse said crossly.

"The mole is handsome and rich. He will make you an excellent husband. Marry him or I will bite you!"

The field mouse told Thumbelina the wedding would take place in a month. Four spiders spun the wedding veil, while Thumbelina sewed her tiny wedding gown.

As the wedding day drew near, Thumbelina became sadder and sadder. How dreadful it would be to always live in the darkness. Would she ever see the blue sky or the bright sun again? Would she ever hear a bird sing?

The day before the wedding, Thumbelina begged the field mouse to let her go outside one last time. At last, the field mouse gave her permission.

Thumbelina slipped out the door and stared longingly at the bright sky.

"Farewell, beautiful sun," she cried, stretching out her arms. "Farewell, sweet flowers! Please say hello to my dear swallow for me if you ever see him again!"

Just then Thumbelina heard a tweet, tweet above her head, and there was the swallow himself! He was flying south for winter, and he had come to say good-bye to Thumbelina before he went.

Thumbelina began to cry. She told him how she was to marry the mole the next day.

"Oh, no," cried the swallow. "Come with me instead. I will fly you to beautiful lands where the sun always shines and flowers always bloom."

"Oh, yes," Thumbelina said, "I will go with you!" for she could not bear to marry the mole.

Quickly she climbed on the swallow's back. Then the bird spread his wings and he and Thumbelina flew away. They flew over tall pine forests and snow-covered mountain peaks to warm countries where the grass is always green and orange and lemon trees grow.

After several days, they came to a clear blue lake. An ancient palace of white marble stood beside it. In the garden lay a marble pillar broken into three pieces.

Large, beautiful flowers were growing among the pieces of pillar. The swallow placed Thumbelina beside the most beautiful flower. "I think you will be happy here," he told her.

Just then the petals opened. Inside was a tiny man with shining gossamer wings. He was the fairy of that flower and king of all the flower fairies. He was just Thumbelina's size, and he fell in love with her at once.

"Will you be my wife?" he asked. Thumbelina smiled, for he was nothing like the horrible mole. "Yes," she said happily.

At that all the flowers opened and each flower fairy gave Thumbelina a gift. The best gift of all was a pair of tiny gossamer wings. Now Thumbelina would be able to fly and flit from flower to flower.

At Thumbelina's wedding to the fairy king, the swallow sang a special wedding song. Then it was time for him to fly back north. As he went he sang of Thumbelina, and that is how we came to hear her story.

MOTHER GOOSE'S
NURSERY RHYMES

Illustrated by ROBYN OFFICER

$\mathcal{H}$ERE WE GO round the mulberry bush,

The mulberry bush, the mulberry bush.

Here we go round the mulberry bush,

On a cold and frosty morning.

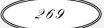

*H*ICKORY, dickory, dock,
The mouse ran up the clock.
The clock struck one,
The mouse ran down,
And hickory, dickory, dock.

*L*ITTLE BO-PEEP *has lost her sheep,*
And doesn't know where to find them.
Leave them alone, and they'll come home,
Dragging their tails behind them.

*S*IMPLE SIMON *met a pieman*
Going to the fair;
Says Simple Simon to the pieman,
Let me taste your ware.

Says the pieman to Simple Simon,
Show me first your penny.
Says Simple Simon to the pieman,
Indeed I have not any.

HEY Diddle, Diddle,
The cat and the fiddle,
The cow jumped over the moon;
The little dog laughed
To see such sport
And the dish ran away with the spoon.

*I*TSY bitsy spider, climbed up the water spout,
Down came the rain and washed poor spider out.
Out came the sun and dried up all the rain;
And the itsy bitsy spider, climbed up the spout again.

*R*ING around the roses,
A pocket full of posies;
Ashes, ashes!
We all fall down.

THREE blind mice, see how they run!
They all ran after the farmer's wife,
Who cut off their tails with a carving knife.
Did you ever see such a sight in your life,
As three blind mice?

*H*UMPTY DUMPTY *sat on a wall,*
Humpty Dumpty had a great fall.
All the king's horses and all the king's men
Couldn't put Humpty Dumpty together again.

*L*ONDON BRIDGE *is falling down,*
Falling down, falling down.
London bridge is falling down,
My fair lady.

$\mathcal{T}$HERE was an old woman who lived in a shoe,
She had so many children she didn't know what to do;
She gave them some broth without any bread;
She whipped them all soundly and put them to bed.

$\mathcal{J}$ACK and Jill went up the hill
To fetch a pail of water;
Jack fell down and broke his crown,
And Jill came tumbling after.

PETER PIPER picked a peck of pickled pepper
A peck of pickled pepper Peter Piper picked.
If Peter Piper picked a peck of pickled pepper,
Where's the peck of pickled pepper Peter Piper picked?

TOM, TOM, *the piper's son,*
Stole a pig and away did run;
The pig was eat, and Tom was beat,
And Tom ran crying down the street.

RUB-*a-dub-dub*,
Three men in a tub,
And who do you think they be?
The butcher, the baker,
The candlestick-maker,
Turn 'em out, knaves all three!

MARY had a little lamb,
Its fleece was white as snow;
And everywhere that Mary went
The lamb was sure to go.

It followed her to school one day,
That was against the rule;
It made the children laugh and play,
To see a lamb in school.

PETER, PETER, *pumpkin eater,*
Had a wife and couldn't keep her;
He put her in a pumpkin shell,
And there he kept her very well.

Peter, Peter, pumpkin eater,
Had another, and didn't love her;
Peter learned to read and spell,
And then he loved her very well.

Puss in Boots

Retold by SAMANTHA EASTON

Illustrated by DEBBIE DIENEMAN

*T*here was once an old miller who had three sons. When the miller died, he left to his sons his mill, his donkey, and his cat. As was the custom, the eldest son inherited the mill. The second son received the donkey, and the third got only the cat.

Now, the third son was very good-natured, and he accepted his inheritance cheerfully. Nevertheless, when he was alone, he could not help sighing, "How

lucky my brothers are! With a mill and a donkey they will be able to live comfortably, but with only a cat I shall surely starve if I do not soon find work!"

To the young man's surprise, the cat, who had been listening from the corner, said, "Do not despair, my good master. I am not as useless as I look. Get me a sack and a pair of leather boots so that I may tramp around the countryside without hurting my paws. Then you shall see what I can do for you."

"A cat that can speak as well as that must be clever," thought the young man. So he took all the money he had and bought the cat a canvas sack and a fine pair of leather boots.

The cat was delighted when he saw the boots and put them on at once.

"My, how fine you look!" said the young man, laughing a little, for the cat looked so pleased with himself. "From now on I shall call you Puss in Boots!"

"You may call me whatever you like," replied the cat. "But now I am off to make your fortune."

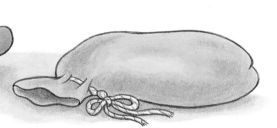

Puss in Boots filled his canvas bag with carrots.
Then he stalked off to a rabbit warren that was full of
plump, young rabbits.

He opened his bag, then stretched out on the
ground beside it and lay very still. Presently some
curious rabbits ran into the bag to eat the carrots. At
once, Puss in Boots leaped up and tied the bag shut
with the rabbits still inside.

Then, feeling very proud of his catch, he went to the palace and asked to see the king himself. The king's servants had never seen a cat wearing fine leather boots before. They were so amazed, they immediately led Puss in Boots to his majesty's throne room.

Puss in Boots bowed low to the king. "Greetings, your majesty," he said. "These rabbits come from my master's warren, and he has asked me to make you a present of them."

"How kind," said the king. "Pray, tell me, what is your master's name?"

"He is the Marquis of Carabas," Puss in Boots replied grandly, though the miller's son was called no such thing.

"Then kindly thank him for me," said the king. "And tell him that I am very pleased."

Puss in Boots said that he would do so and returned home.

The next day, Puss in Boots filled his canvas bag with corn. Then he went to a place in the country where many wild pheasants nested. Opening the bag wide, he stretched out beside it and lay very still. Presently, a number of pheasants ran inside to eat the corn. Then Puss in Boots quickly tied the bag shut and once again went to the king.

Puss in Boots bowed low before his majesty and

said, "My lord, the Marquis of Carabas has asked me to give you these pheasants as a token of his esteem."

"My, how very thoughtful!" said the king. "I only hope someday I can repay your master's kindness."

Puss in Boots was very glad to hear this. When he had bid good-bye to the king, he rushed home to the miller's son.

"Listen, master," Puss in Boots said that night, "I have a plan that will make your fortune. Tomorrow morning I will take you to a place along the river where you will go swimming. Do as I say and I will take care of the rest."

The miller's son could not understand how this would make his fortune. But he thought, "The cat certainly seems to know what he is doing." So he agreed to do as Puss in Boots had asked.

Early the next morning Puss in Boots led the miller's son to a part of the river that ran beside the king's palace. Then the miller's son went swimming, leaving his clothes on the bank.

Puss in Boots hid his master's clothes under a rock. Then he shouted as loudly as he could, "Help! Help! My master, the Marquis of Carabas, is about to be drowned!"

Now, as Puss in Boots knew quite well, the king walked along that part of the river every morning. Sure enough, soon the king came walking down the road with his daughter, the princess. When he heard Puss in Boots' cries, he ordered his guards to leap into the river at once and save the Marquis of Carabas.

While the guards were pulling the miller's son to shore, Puss in Boots told the king that wicked robbers had set upon his master and stolen all his clothes.

"How terrible!" cried the king. Then he ordered his servants to fetch one of his best suits of clothes for the unfortunate Marquis to wear.

When the miller's son was dressed in royal clothes, he looked so handsome that the princess instantly fell in love with him.

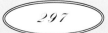

Puss in Boots watched how the princess smiled at the miller's son. This was just what he had hoped would happen. He took his master aside and whispered, "Tell the king and the princess that if only your carriage hadn't been stolen, you would gladly invite them to see your palace to repay them for their kindness."

"What are you saying?" the miller's son cried. "I have no palace!"

"Do as I tell you," said Puss in Boots. "And you shall soon have the princess for a wife."

Now, the miller's son had fallen as much in love with the princess as she had with him. So he eagerly agreed, although he could not imagine what his cat intended to do.

The king was very pleased by the invitation and quickly accepted. "My daughter and I would be overjoyed to go visit your palace," the king exclaimed. "We shall go there at once in my carriage!" So Puss in Boots gave the king's coachman instructions, and they prepared to set out.

While the king and the princess and the miller's son waited for the carriage to be made ready, Puss in Boots ran ahead.

Down the road he came upon a group of people mowing a large meadow. Puss in Boots called to them in a mournful voice, "Oh, my good people, be careful or you will surely lose your heads today!"

"What do you mean?" asked one of them.

"The king is coming with his guards," said Puss in Boots. "He will stop and ask you to whom this meadow belongs. You must answer the Marquis of

Carabas, for if you do not the king's soldiers will chop off your heads at once!"

"Never fear," replied one of the men. "We will do so without fail!"

Soon the king came passing by. When he saw the large meadow, he ordered the carriage to stop. "Tell me, my good people," he asked, "to whom does this meadow belong?"

"Why, sir! To the Marquis of Carabas!" they all replied at once.

"Ah," said the king, looking very pleased. "A very fine meadow it is, too." And he ordered the carriage to move on.

Meanwhile Puss in Boots had run on ahead. Presently, he came to a huge field of corn where people were busy harvesting. Puss in Boots stopped and called to them in a gloomy voice. "Oh, my good people," he cried, "please be very, very careful today. Otherwise, I fear you will surely lose your heads!"

"What are you saying?" they asked.

"The king is coming with all his guards," replied Puss in Boots. "He will ask you to whom this field of corn belongs. You must answer 'To the Marquis of Carabas.' If you don't—well, you can imagine what the king's men will do then!"

"Don't worry," said one of the workers. "We will certainly give the king the answer he wants!"

So when the king came by a moment later and asked the workers to whom the great cornfield belonged, they all replied at once, "Why, to the Marquis of Carabas, your majesty!"

And on it went. Every time the king passed something and asked to whom it belonged, the answer was always the same: "This belongs to the Marquis of Carabas, your majesty!"

Meanwhile, Puss in Boots kept going until he came to an enormous stone castle. This castle belonged to a wicked ogre. The ogre was very rich— and the actual owner of all the fields the king's carriage had passed.

Puss in Boots knocked on the door. When the ogre's servants answered, Puss in Boots asked to be taken to see their master at once. The servants had never seen a cat wearing boots before so they led him straight to the ogre's room.

Puss in Boots bowed low. "I have come to pay my respects," he said, "for I have heard that you are a very remarkable person!"

"So I am," said the ogre.

"I have even been told," Puss in Boots went on, "that you can turn yourself into any creature in the world—even a proud lion! However, I do not believe how this can possibly be true."

"Don't you?" cried the ogre, most insulted. Then to prove his powers, he turned himself into a great roaring lion.

"How remarkable," said Puss in Boots, taking a

step backward, for he was rather afraid of lions. "You truly amaze me! I have also been told that you can turn yourself into a tiny mouse. But I am sure that is quite impossible!"

"Impossible?" roared the ogre. "Just watch!" Then, quick as a wink, he turned himself into a little gray mouse and scampered across the floor.

Puss in Boots wasted no time. He quickly pounced on the tiny mouse and ate him up!

Just then the king's carriage drew up to the palace gates. Puss in Boots dusted himself off and ran outside to meet them.

As the king and the princess stepped down from the carriage, Puss in Boots hailed them, "Welcome, your majesty, to the home of my lord and master, the Marquis of Carabas!"

The miller's son was very surprised, but he quickly recovered himself and showed his guests inside.

All the servants clapped and cheered, "Long live the Marquis of Carabas!" The wicked ogre had treated them very badly, and they were happy to have a new master.

The king was quite impressed with the palace and thought to himself that the Marquis of Carabas must be a wealthy, powerful man. So he offered his daughter's hand in marriage to the happy miller's son.

The beautiful princess and the Marquis of Carabas were married that day, and a splendid wedding it was!

The two of them lived together very happily for many long years.

As for Puss in Boots, his master made him a lord. And he never had to chase mice again— unless he chose to, of course!

AESOP'S

TABLES

Retold by FIONA BLACK

Illustrated by RICHARD BERNAL

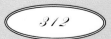

THE HARE AND THE TORTOISE

A hare was always making fun of a tortoise for being so slow. "Get moving, slowpoke," he would shout. "Is that the fastest you can go?" One day, the tortoise decided that he had had enough and challenged the hare to a race.

The hare laughed and laughed. "A race with you?" he scoffed. "I'll get to the finish before you even cross the starting line!"

"Never mind that," said the tortoise. "Let's just have the race."

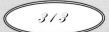

A course was set by all the animals and the fox was to be the judge. When the fox barked, the race began.

Quicker than you can say "Go," the hare sprang ahead and vanished down the path. Meanwhile the tortoise went along at his usual slow speed.

Before long, the hare decided to stop and have a rest. "After all," he thought, "that slow tortoise will take hours to catch up with me!"

So he stretched out on some shady grass. Soon he began to yawn. "Perhaps I'll just take a quick nap," he said, and with that, he fell asleep.

Meanwhile the tortoise kept plodding along. And when the hare awoke, the tortoise was at the finish line.

So the moral of the story is as follows: In the end, slow and steady wins the race.

THE FOX AND THE GRAPES

A hungry fox was walking one day when he saw some ripe grapes hanging from a vine. The fox leaped up for the nearest bunch and snapped his jaws, but he missed. He tried again and again, but the grapes were just out of reach. At last, he slunk off, muttering, "I never wanted those grapes, anyway. They are probably sour!"

This story teaches us that it is all too easy to scorn the things we cannot have.

THE OAK AND THE REED

A mighty oak tree grew by a river. One day a fierce storm knocked the tree down. After the storm ended, the oak tree was amazed to see the river reeds still standing, and he asked them how this was possible.

"It is simple," one reed replied. "When the wind came, you were too proud to bend even a little. But I know I am only a humble reed. So when the wind blew, I bent over. That is why I am still here."

And so we learn that it is better to bend than to break.

ANDROCLES AND THE LION

There once was a slave named Androcles whose master treated him cruelly. Androcles could bear it no longer, and one day he ran away into the forest. There he came upon a roaring lion. At first he was frightened, but then he saw that the lion was crying from pain.

As Androcles drew near, the lion put out its paw. Androcles saw a large thorn in one of the lion's toes and pulled it out.

The lion was so grateful, it licked Androcles' hand and led him to its cave. Androcles remained with the lion for some time, and every day the lion caught game for them to eat.

One day, as Androcles and the lion were hunting together, they were both captured. They were taken to the city and put in a circus. For entertainment, Androcles was to be thrown to a lion that had not been fed for several days to make it as fierce and hungry as possible. The emperor himself was coming to watch the show.

On the day of the event, Androcles was led to the center of the arena. Then the lion was let out of its cage. With a terrible roar, it bounded toward the poor slave.

As the snarling lion drew near Androcles, it suddenly stopped, rolled over, and licked his hand. The emperor was so impressed by the unusual sight that he called Androcles before him to explain. When Androcles told the emperor the whole story, the emperor set him free. He also set the lion free to return to the forest.

And so this story teaches us that a good deed never goes unrewarded.

THE FOX AND THE CROW

Once a crow stole a piece of cheese and flew to a treetop to enjoy her prize. A fox caught sight of her, and thought to himself, "If I am clever and act quickly, I shall have that cheese for my supper!"

So he sat under the tree and began to speak to the crow in his softest and most polite tone of voice. "Good day, Mistress Crow," he began. "How fine you look today! Your feathers are so glossy and black, and your claws look so strong.

"Why, you look like a queen perched there on that branch," the fox crooned. "I only wish that I could hear your voice, for I am certain that it must be every bit as beautiful as the rest of you!"

The vain crow was delighted, for she believed his every word. She nodded her head and flapped her wings with joy. She was especially pleased that the fox had praised her voice, for she had often been told that her caw was rather harsh. So, thinking to impress the fox with her lovely voice, she opened her beak wide.

Down fell the cheese right into the fox's open jaws! As the fox trotted away, licking his lips, he called to the crow, "Next time someone flatters you, you would do well to be more cautious!"

And so we learn from the tale of the fox and the crow that flatterers are not to be trusted!

THE UGLY DUCKLING

By HANS CHRISTIAN ANDERSEN

Retold by JENNIFER GREENWAY

Illustrated by ROBYN OFFICER

One lovely summer day, on the bank of a quiet pond beside an old farmhouse, a duck sat on her nest waiting for her eggs to hatch.

First a crack appeared on one egg, then on another, and another. Little ducklings began to poke their heads out of the shells.

The mother duck was delighted until she noticed that one egg still had not hatched. This egg was larger than the others and a dull gray color.

The mother duck sighed. She was about to sit on the nest awhile longer when one of the older ducks in the pond came by. She asked the mother duck about her ducklings and then said, "I wouldn't bother trying to hatch that egg if I were you. It looks like a turkey egg to me. I hatched one once by mistake, and it

caused me no end of trouble. Leave that egg alone and come teach your ducklings to swim!"

But the mother duck replied that she had been sitting on her nest so long already, a little more time wouldn't matter. And she settled onto her nest and waited patiently.

Presently, the mother duck heard a sharp crack, and out popped the last duckling. But what a strange duckling he was! He was twice as big as the others, and had gray feathers instead of yellow.

Even his mother had to admit he was rather ugly. "Oh, dear," she thought. "Perhaps it was a turkey egg after all!"

The next morning, she led her ducklings to the pond to teach them how to swim. The ugly duckling jumped right in the water and swam with no trouble.

"Well, he can't be a turkey, if he can swim as well as that," his mother said to herself. "Besides, if you look at him properly, he isn't so ugly!"

Feeling very proud, the mother duck called her ducklings out of the water. Then she led them to the barnyard to introduce them to the other ducks.

"Be sure to behave yourselves," she told them as they walked through the grass. "And don't forget to say 'quack' and bow politely to everyone."

In the barnyard, the ducklings did as they were told. They bowed politely to everyone and said "quack." The other ducks looked them over carefully. "Your ducklings are all very well behaved," one of the old ducks said at last. "And they are all very pretty— except for that big gray one. He is the ugliest duckling I've ever seen!"

All the other ducks in the barnyard agreed, and even the ugly duckling's brothers and sisters began to make fun of him.

"He is ugly," replied his mother, "but he is clever and polite and means no harm."

"Very well," sniffed the other ducks. "He can stay, so long as he stays out of sight."

The other ducklings quickly made themselves at home. But from that moment on, everyone in the barnyard was mean to the ugly duckling. His brothers and sisters kicked him and bit him. The older ducks chased him. The hens and roosters pecked him. One day, even his mother admitted that she wished he had never been born.

When he heard that, the ugly duckling decided to run away, and he flew over the hedge and into the fields. He soon came to the marsh where the wild ducks lived, and there he fell asleep.

When he awoke, the wild ducks were standing around him, staring curiously.

"What are you?" they said. "We have never seen a duck like you before."

"I don't know myself," replied the ugly duckling shyly.

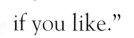

"It is only that you are so very ugly!" said the wild ducks. "But you seem nice enough, so you may stay with us if you like."

The grateful ugly duckling flew with the wild ducks over the marsh. Suddenly there were loud popping sounds. Hunters in the marsh below were firing their guns at the wild ducks! The poor ducks all dropped into the water—dead.

The ugly duckling was terrified and hid among the reeds. A hunting dog ran past him, baring his fangs. But the dog did not stop.

"Ah," the ugly duckling thought sadly. "I am so ugly that even a dog won't bite me." He sat very still until the hunters left. Then he flew alone toward the forest.

The ugly duckling flew until he was so tired that he could hardly flap his wings. It was evening by then, and a storm was gathering. Soon rain began to fall. Cold and hungry, the ugly duckling was happy to see the light of a cottage ahead. He flew toward it, and, finding the door open, he went inside.

The cottage belonged to an old woman who lived there with her big tomcat and her prize red hen. When they saw the ugly duckling, the hen began to cluck and the cat began to hiss.

"What is it?" cried the old woman, who was very nearsighted. When she caught sight of the ugly duckling she thought he was a nice fat duck who had run away from a nearby farm. "Oh, good!" she said. "Now I shall have duck's eggs to eat." She fed the ugly duckling some bread and water and told him he could stay if he liked.

This did not please the cat or the hen at all, for they liked to think that they were master and mistress of the household. After the old woman had gone to bed, they turned on the ugly duckling.

"Can you lay eggs?" clucked the hen.

"No," replied the ugly duckling.

"Can you arch your back and purr?" hissed the cat.

"No," replied the ugly duckling.

"Then what good are you?" said the cat.

"Can't you do anything at all?" said the hen.

"I can swim," replied the ugly duckling. Then he told them how lovely the water felt and what fun it was to dive to the bottom.

"Fun?" cried the hen. "Why, it sounds horrible!"

"Dreadful!" agreed the cat. "You had better learn to purr or lay eggs, or you won't be here much longer."

Then the cat scratched the ugly duckling, and the hen pecked him, until the poor creature decided he had better leave.

So the ugly duckling flew to a quiet pond in the middle of the forest. There, he could swim and dive all day long. But he was careful to hide from all the other creatures, because he had grown ashamed of his ugliness.

Autumn came. Leaves fell from the trees and the wind grew sharp. The days were growing shorter, and the nights were getting colder. It would soon be winter. It was becoming harder to find food, and the ugly duckling was hungry and lonely.

One cool evening, he was resting at the edge of the pond and gazing at the sunset, when he saw a great flock of birds flying overhead.

The birds were the most beautiful the ugly duckling had ever seen. They were white as snow with wide, strong wings and long, graceful necks. The ugly duckling did not know it, but these were swans flying south for the winter. Suddenly, they spread their wings and all together uttered a cry unlike anything the ugly duckling had ever heard. Then they flew on, their feathers gleaming in the last rays of the sun.

The ugly duckling stared after them. Then without realizing it, he arched his neck and called back to them—a cry so strange it frightened him. No living creature had ever made him feel that way before. How he wished he could be as lovely as those proud, white birds were! "But what would such royal birds say if they were to see me?" he thought sadly.

Soon cruel winter came. The ugly duckling had to swim in a circle all day to keep the pond from freezing over. Each day, the circle in which he could swim grew smaller and smaller. One day, it was so cold that, despite the ugly duckling's efforts, the pond completely froze. The poor ugly duckling could not swim another stroke, and he fell exhausted on the ice.

The next morning, a peasant passing by saw the ugly duckling lying on the ice. Feeling sorry for him, the peasant picked up the poor little bird and carried him home.

His wife put the ugly duckling next to the fire. Soon he warmed up and began to spread his wings. When the peasant's children saw this, they came running toward him, for they wanted to play with the duckling.

The ugly duckling was so frightened that he beat his wings, knocking over the milk jug. Then he flew into the butter cask and then into the barrel of cornmeal. After that, the ugly duckling looked a sight!

The woman screamed and chased him with a broom. The children fell over each other trying to catch him. The ugly duckling barely managed to escape through the window!

The rest of that winter was lonely and difficult for the ugly duckling.

Then one day, he awoke to find the warm sun shining. Green leaves were budding on the trees. Beautiful spring had come at last! Joyfully, the ugly duckling spread his wings and flew. Soon he came to a pond.

Three proud swans were gliding across the water. When the ugly duckling saw them, he felt sadder than ever. "I will swim over to those beautiful, proud birds," he thought. "I am so ugly, they will surely kill me. But it will be better to be killed by them, than be bitten by ducks and pecked by hens and hated by everyone."

So he swam toward them with his head down to show he was prepared to die. It was then that the ugly duckling saw his reflection in the water. Instead of an ugly gray bird, he was snow-white with a long graceful neck. The ugly duckling had grown into a beautiful swan!

The three swans swam to him and stroked his neck with their beaks in welcome. Just then some children came running up to the edge of the pond. "Look!" they cried. "A new swan! Why, he is the most beautiful one of all!"

The once ugly duckling shyly ruffled his feathers and thought, "When I was the ugly duckling, I never dreamed I would ever be so happy!"

The text of this book was set in Goudy and the

display in Swanson by Harry Chester, Inc.,

New York City

Book design by Judith Stagnitto Abbate